CH01455101

# MAN OF THE MONTH CLUB: MAY

SPICY ENEMIES-TO-LOVERS, OPPOSITES
ATTRACT MATCHMAKER ROMANCE

ANN OMASTA

CALLIE LOVE

# FREE BOOK!

**Have you met sexy, magnetic, and heroic Ranger? He's the total package... and it's a big one!**

*His First Time: Ranger* is FREE when you join Callie Love's VIP reader group. It's a reader group <u>EXCLUSIVE</u> and isn't available anywhere else. We value your privacy and never send spam. Just visit callielove.com and tell us where to send your Hot Shot of Romance Quickie freebie.

# DEDICATION

*Thank you, Mom, for the wonderful
handwritten notes you left behind
documenting your hilarious, playful 'insult
wars' with your granddaughter. You always
had the best sense of humor, and I'm so glad
you passed that love of silliness and laughter
on to her.*

*Poppy and Cooper borrowed a few of your
comedic gems for their bickering because your
creative, loving jabs at each other are far
superior to anything we could make up.*

*I miss you every single day and wish I could
give you the biggest hug ever. I love you.*

## POPPY

*I* glance away from the road for a second to wink at my friend, Daphne. "You have nothing to worry about. Everyone likes you. I'm the one who speaks my mind without a filter and ends up leaving a trail of enemies in my wake."

"You do not," Daphne assures me in her soft voice. "Anyone who takes the time to get to know the real you, loves you."

I appreciate her sweet sentiment, even if it's not exactly true.

When I weave quickly into the left lane of the I-465 beltway that loops Indianapolis, Daphne sucks in an audible breath before saying, "I don't think I'll ever get used to this traffic."

As we pass a long line of semis, I say,

"You just gotta take the bull by the horns and jump in, my friend. If you want something, take it. That philosophy works for both driving and life in general."

Although it's sage advice, I know my shy friend will never be assertive. It's not in her nature, but she has Ben and me to stick up for her, if anyone ever tries to bother her.

Daphne is staring down at her lap as she says, "I just don't want the other women to think I shouldn't be at the meeting, since I already found my love match."

"What are you talking about? You are a smashing success story that makes all of the rest of us want to find what you have. Besides, Phoebe removes past matches from the pool of surveys, so it's not like you'll affect anyone's likelihood of being selected."

"I guess so," Daphne agrees as I angle my small car onto the off-ramp and head towards Evie's Bar & Grill.

The parking lot for the bar is packed. "I guess the competition is going to be fierce tonight."

"Word about the success of the application must be spreading like wildfire," Daphne guesses.

When I see the reverse lights on the

small SUV just ahead of us, I put my compact car into reverse. Once I back up enough to give me room to slide into the spot, I shift the car back into drive.

Daphne's voice is shaky when she says, "I think that car sitting over there with its turn signal on has been waiting for this spot."

"Well, with any luck, we're going to swoop in and get it before Mr. Mercedes even knows what happened," I assure her.

It's obvious Daphne is not on board with this plan when she says, "Can't we just park someplace else? I think there's a parking garage a couple of blocks away. I'll be happy to pay for it."

"Nonsense. There's a perfectly good spot right here beside the bar," I tell her.

"But that man isn't going to be happy if we take the place he's been waiting for," Daphne squeaks.

Ignoring her, I gun my Mini Cooper forward as soon as the SUV reverses and stops to change gears. There's just enough room in front of the SUV for me to squeeze my car into the newly available spot while the schmuck in the Mercedes, waiting with his turning signal on behind the SUV, sits there unable to move.

A horn blasts, so I say under my breath, "Sore loser."

"I don't like this," Daphne says nervously.

"We won fair and square," I tell her as I reach into the back seat to grab my purse before opening my door to emerge.

The Mercedes is sitting directly behind my car. The driver rolls down the passenger's side window to yell, "Didn't you see me waiting for that spot with my turn signal on?"

"Oh, I saw... But you snooze, you lose," I yell back, completely unimpressed by his fancy car or his dashing good looks.

"Unbelievable," he mutters and shakes his head.

As he revs his engine and drives away, I turn to give Daphne a wide, reassuring smile. "Ready?"

"I guess so," she answers, seeming completely rattled by the interaction--even though she wasn't directly involved.

Once inside the crowded bar, I find us some chairs and scoot them up to the lively group's table, forcing them to make room for us.

A couple of the ladies aren't shy about glaring at me--likely over last month's harmless April Fools' prank. Determined not to be intimidated by them, I say, "You have to put up with me to get Daphne, and she's a delight."

Wide-eyed gazes greet my bold statement. Finally, someone begins giggling. Soon, the entire table erupts with laughter, making it obvious I have effectively broken the ice.

Phoebe glances up and says to someone, who has evidently walked up behind my chair, "Great timing. Everyone, meet May's Man of the Month, Cooper Bridgerton."

I turn and look up into the gleaming sapphire eyes of Mr. Mercedes.

He narrows a fierce, icy glare down at me as recognition sets in. His lip curls just before he says in a deep growl, "You…"

# COOPER

*I* had been hoping to arrive at the bar early, so I could find a quiet corner where I could remain unnoticed as I checked out the group of ladies. But the rude woman in the sporty Mini Cooper had ruined that grand plan. I'd been forced to park at a garage three blocks away and speed-walk here to make it at the agreed-upon time. I hate being late–– or even almost late.

When the woman from the parking lot altercation looks up at me with innocence and sunshine shining in her eyes, I'm determined to remain angry with her. She might be gorgeous and confident, but she's also selfish and impolite.

The tiny hairs on the back of my neck bristle as I glare down at her. I want to tell her off or kiss her senseless, and both of those urges piss me off. I'm not normally an angry person, so for her to cause this kind of volatile reaction within me is unsettling.

Deciding it's in my best interest to ignore her and hope that we never have to see each other again, I turn my attention to the other lovely women at the table. When I lock eyes with the raven-haired beauty sitting beside the ill-mannered woman, I'm left with very little doubt about her identity.

"Daphne?" I ask her before lifting the back of her hand to my lips.

She smiles and says, "Yes, I'm so thrilled to finally meet you, Cooper."

I take note of the 'finally' she tosses into the sentence. My brother, Ben, has been trying to arrange a dinner for us to meet, but I keep having urgent work situations arise that force me to cancel. For some reason, people seem to think their money––and my managing of it––should take precedence over any kind of social commitment I may have.

Hoping to charm her into forgiving me, I say, "It's easy to see why Ben has fallen head-over-heels for you."

The delightful woman actually blushes. It's a charming and sweet reaction that so rarely happens naturally these days. I'd be willing to bet the ball-buster who drove Daphne here hasn't blushed in years––if ever.

Not wanting to focus all of my attention on Daphne, since she's already spoken for by Ben, I turn to scan the rest of the table. I plaster a wide smile on my face and make eye contact with each woman, until I reach the end of the circle. I purposely skip over Daphne's obnoxious friend, opting instead to turn toward Phoebe, who has been friends with my brother since grade school.

The astute woman quickly picks up on my cue and resumes her role as announcer for the group. "As most of you know, Cooper is Ben's older brother. I've known him for years and can vouch that he's quite a catch, beyond his astounding good looks."

Phoebe's gaze darts away from mine as she makes the compliment. I've never thought about her in a romantic capacity because she was always merely one of my little brother's pesky friends, but suddenly I'm seeing her in a new light. She's all grown up now, and she has matured into a beautiful, bright woman.

Feeling frisky, I wink at her as soon as she glances back at me. I wonder if she might be my compatibility match and begin to hope that she is. It would probably irk Ben for a bit, which would make it even more fun. Besides, he can't begrudge us finding happiness together, since he is now madly in love with Daphne.

Phoebe tucks her hair behind her ear as she uncharacteristically struggles to find words. "So, umm, yeah. Cooper is a successful businessman with a great personality. And, uh... being Ben's brother means he's also a Bridgerton."

The ladies go wild at this revelation––squealing and whispering to each other.

It's all I can do to keep from rolling my eyes. That blasted show is making my last name a curse. Women practically swoon upon hearing it, until they realize I'm not actually a devilish duke or even a valorous viscount.

Once the commotion dies down over my surname, Phoebe resumes her speech. "The woman selected as Cooper's match is one lucky lady. In fact, I'm a bit jealous."

Her revelation steals away the hope that Phoebe might announce her own name. I give her a sad half-smile as she continues. "The most compatible lady for Coop is..."

The women take her pause as their cue

to begin hammering their palms on the table to create a drumroll.

Phoebe draws out the moment, allowing the suspense to build, before announcing, "For the second month in a row, Poppy Pendleton!"

I look around trying to figure out which one of these beauties is named Poppy. All eyes turn toward the shrew beside Daphne. I take an involuntary step backward, unable to believe my rotten luck. I would prefer to go out with any other woman at this table––with the possible exception of Daphne, since my brother would kill me for that.

Poppy turns a startled gaze up at me before holding her palms up and addressing the table at large in a loud voice, "I swear, I didn't rig the results this time around."

When she grabs her handbag and hops down from her stool, I glare down at her before saying, "I know you don't think I'm taking you on a date."

## 3

## POPPY

*H*umiliation surges through my veins as I stand there holding my purse, like a dope, and gaping at the man who just insulted me in front of everyone. There's no denying we got off to a rocky start in the parking lot, but I never dreamed he would shun me like this after we were matched by the app's algorithm.

"Cooper!" Phoebe hisses, chastising the man's open rudeness.

He turns wide eyes to her. Sounding defensive, he asks, "What? She's awful. She can't possibly be my best love match out of all of these wonderful candidates."

Trying to save face, I climb back onto my bar stool and say, "It's fine if you want to bow out from your commitment. I can be a lot to handle. It sounds like you're not strong or confident enough to take me on."

I take a sip from the straw of my drink, hoping that my cheeks and neck aren't as red as they feel.

"Oh, I could handle you, I just don't care to," he informs me, sounding super cocky.

Ignoring him, I turn to Phoebe and say, "Perhaps Cooper should go out with his next-best match."

Phoebe shakes her head as she says, "You two are meant to be a pair. I'd bet my reputation on it. The runner-up isn't even a true compatibility match with him."

Ever the peace-keeper, Daphne turns to look up at Cooper. Although she speaks softly, everyone listens. "Phoebe's app has made four successful matches in a row. Aren't you at least curious to see if it's right about you and Poppy?"

I'm curious, but I would never admit that aloud, since he has just publicly rejected me.

Cooper shakes his head. "It can't be right. She is the one woman at this table I *didn't* want to be matched with."

"Oh, that's what it is, then." Summer, the woman on my other side, weighs in with authority. "You were focused on your fear of being matched with Poppy, so the Universe delivered. It always brings you what you ask for with your dominant thoughts and feelings, so you should try to pay attention to what you *do* want, rather than what you don't wish to happen."

This woo-woo mumbo jumbo is hogwash, but several women around the table nod their heads as if the loon beside me is making sense. At least her rambling is keeping everyone's focus off my shame at being so harshly denied.

Daphne brightens with an idea. Turning to Cooper she asks, "How about if I call Ben and have him meet us somewhere? It will give you and me a chance to get to know each other. Plus, you and Poppy can see if you have a connection, without the pressure of a one-on-one date."

Cooper's expression softens. I know from experience that Daphne is impossible to resist when she turns those sweet, innocent eyes toward you. Proving the truth in that, Cooper relents, "I suppose that might work."

Although I appreciate my friend's effort, it's beyond embarrassing that the man is having to be convinced to go out on a date with me, so I snap, "Don't do me any favors."

"If I go, it's because I've been trying to find time to get to know my brother's girlfriend, not because I want to spend time with you."

"Understood," I say crisply, trying not to reveal how hurt I am by his angry words and scowl. Feeling the need to stick up for myself, I add, "I don't particularly want to go out with you, either."

"Good," he grouches.

"Great," I answer back, determined to one-up him.

Ignoring our childish bickering, Daphne claps her hands and says, "Yay! A double date will be so much fun. I'll call Ben right now."

While she's taking care of that, things turn awkward at the table. Cooper is the first man of the month to not be delighted to whisk his lady out of here––except for when Ben thought I was his match. Apparently, the Bridgerton men are simply not into me.

The women are staring at me with wide eyes, so after taking another sip of my drink, I say, "I can be a bit of an acquired taste."

Cooper scoffs behind me, but refrains from commenting.

Soon, Daphne rejoins us at the table and says, "Ben is going to meet us at Wendy's just up the road, if that's okay? I've been dying to try a Frosty."

I grin at my best friend. She's lived such a sheltered life until now, that she is easily impressed by simple things that most of us take for granted.

Cooper seems taken aback by the suggestion that we get fast food as he croaks, "Wendy's?"

"That sounds terrific," I assure Daphne, before turning to look up at Cooper to add, "Unless you're too much of a prima donna to eat a cheeseburger and fries?"

Obviously unwilling to let me look like the better person, Cooper holds his hand out to assist Daphne down from the tall bar stool she just sat back down on as he says, "Not at all. In fact, that sounds delicious. Shall we?"

Daphne accepts his offered hand and stands. When he gallantly offers her his elbow to escort her out, she gives me an uncertain look. I shrug my shoulders, trying not to care that my date is more interested in impressing my friend than me.

Turning to the group, Cooper gives them a wave and says, "Ladies, it has been a pleasure. Until next time..."

The women yell out goodbyes and well-wishes for our date as Cooper leads Daphne away from the table. I remain frozen in place, stung that he's completely ignoring me.

When Summer lightly nudges my arm, I move to stand up. Cooper and Daphne are already almost to the door of the bar when I mutter under my breath, "No, no… Don't worry about me. I'll catch up."

With a frustrated huff, I follow the blasted man and my best friend outside.

4

## COOPER

*O*nce we are outside on the sidewalk, I say to Daphne in a voice loud enough for Poppy to overhear, "My car is several blocks away, and I don't particularly want to ride with Poppy. It's a lovely evening. How about if we walk to Wendy's?"

Daphne turns toward her friend to get her opinion, obviously uncomfortable with how I'm treating the other woman. I know I'm being a jerk, but I can't seem to help it. Something about Poppy fires me up beyond reason. It's maddening.

At Poppy's ambivalent shrug of her shoulders, Daphne answers, "Walking sounds wonderful. I just love getting fresh air. Don't you?"

I nod as I wheel her around toward the restaurant and begin walking at a slow pace. Poppy trails along behind us, until Daphne turns back to say, "Come up here with us."

Left with the choice of walking on my free side or beside her best friend, Poppy chooses Daphne. Once the three of us are in alignment, it strikes me how this would look to an outside observer. Since my elbow is locked with Daphne's, it would be logical to assume that she is my date and Poppy is the third wheel.

Hopefully, Ben won't drive by us and see this, or I'll have some explaining to do. Obviously, I'm not interested in stealing my brother's girlfriend, but I'm even less interested in getting to know her obnoxious best friend.

We arrive safely at the restaurant without being spotted by my brother. Once we're inside, we stare up at the menu. Daphne sounds truly astounded when she says, "Everything looks and smells delicious. How are we ever going to decide?"

From anyone else, her words would sound sarcastic or cheesy, but Daphne's childlike wonder is contagious. Just as I'm getting ready to answer, my brother walks up behind her, wraps his arms around her and says, "Try one of each."

She turns and beams up at him before

saying, "I can't do that, but we can come back here again, right?"

"Absolutely," he assures her.

Evidently liking his answer, she tips up onto the balls of her feet to press a sweet kiss to his lips. Ben keeps his face close to hers as he stares down at her with a loving gaze that I've never seen him shower on anyone. It's obvious that if we weren't in public, the two of them would be all over each other.

Poppy rolls her eyes before grouching, "Get a room."

At her sarcastic comment, the two of them reluctantly pull apart, but Ben keeps a possessive arm locked around Daphne's shoulders.

When we are called up to the counter to order, Poppy goes first. She pulls out her wallet to pay, so I step forward to add my order on to hers.

"I can pay for my own food," she tells me firmly.

"I know, but since this is officially a date, I should buy," I offer.

She immediately fires back, "But you don't even want to be here."

I can't deny the truth in that. As I try to think of a comeback, Ben steps forward to say, "Tell you what... Both of you get whatever you want, and I'll pay."

"Don't go overboard, big spender," I tease my kid brother, trying to ease the awkwardness that normally accompanies any money discussions that happen between us. I'm financially successful by most measures, but thanks to Ben's wildly popular comic strip and its merchandising deals, he is a multi-millionaire. As the older, more responsible brother, I had always assumed that I would be the one making the big bucks, so it smarts that Ben is in a completely different league money-wise––even though I try to be happy for him.

"You can buy next time, when we go someplace more expensive," he teases me, effectively releasing the tension.

"Gee, thanks," I mutter good-naturedly.

Once we have our trays of food, we find a table and sit down. Daphne is overjoyed as she dives into her bacon cheeseburger, and she isn't shy about making ecstatic noises and groans as she relishes it.

Ben gives her a half-lidded, desirous gaze as he murmurs, "It should be illegal for you to be this sexy."

Poppy and I make eye contact for the first time since sitting down. When she rolls her eyes over our sappy, romantic tablemates, I nod my head in agreement.

Ben and Daphne only have eyes for each other. After the silence drags on for a bit, Poppy finally says, "Cooper and I can be nauseatingly romantic, too." As proof, she lifts a long French fry up to show us before gazing into my eyes to say, "You remind me of this nasty black spot in my otherwise perfect fry."

The surprised chuckle emerges from my belly before I even realize it's coming. Wanting to join in the ridiculous game, I lean in to say to her, "You're just like the melted ice in my cola."

Poppy chuckles at my quick response before zinging, "You're the air leak in my tire."

"Aww, you're the sweat stain on my white T-shirt," I tell her.

Poppy's eyes are sparkling, making it obvious she's enjoying our insult lobbing as much as I am. She bats her eyelashes dramatically and reaches over to take my hand in her cold one before saying, "You're the worm in my apple."

"You know these aren't romantic at all, right?" Daphne asks.

I had nearly forgotten the two of them were here. When I glance in their direction and see the appalled expressions on their faces, I tip my head back and laugh before turning back to Poppy to say, "You're the pee drop on my toilet seat."

"Eww!" Daphne screeches at the same time as Poppy nods her head, grinning at me as she says, "Nice one!"

I sit back, rather proud of myself, until she fires back, "You're the gum on the bottom of my shoe."

As I scramble to think of another one, enjoying myself immensely, Poppy asks me, "Give up?"

"Never. I could go all night," I assure her.

"We'll see about that," she murmurs in a husky voice that almost sounds flirtatious.

## 5

## POPPY

*T*his is by far the strangest date I've ever been on, but it's also really fun. It's obvious that Daphne and Ben don't understand the pleasure of thinking of creative insults to toss at each other, but I can tell by the way Cooper is leaning in with his bright blue eyes sparkling in my direction that he's enjoying himself as much as I am.

When he calls me 'the mold on his bread,' I tell him he's the 'crack in my mirror.' He responds that I'm the 'commercial during his television show,' so I say he's the 'smushy strawberry at the bottom of my container.' He tosses back that I'm the 'bug guts on his windshield,' so I say he's the 'bill in my mailbox.'

Ben jumps in to say, "Okay, it's obvious that you're both very good at insulting each other. Clearly, you don't enjoy each other's company, so let's call it an evening and mark one strike against Phoebe's matchmaking app."

Cooper gives his brother a startled look as if he has forgotten the other couple is here before asking, "Who says we're not enjoying ourselves? I'm having a fantastic time. How about you, Poppy?"

The admission and question both startle me. I'm surprised to find that I am actually enjoying myself––a great deal. Nodding my head in agreement, I say, "Yes, I'm having a blast. This is more fun than I've had on a date in years."

I hadn't intended for the glowing praise to slip out, but Cooper looks thrilled by the compliment. We turn our attention to Ben when he makes a scoffing noise in his throat. He shakes his head as if he's bewildered by us before saying, "Whatever floats your boat, I guess. But we're out of here, right, Daph?"

"Yes, I'm ready to go home and make love with you," Daphne says as she scrapes her plastic spoon along the bottom of her paper cup to get the last bit of chocolate Frosty out of it.

Her bold honesty is a bit disconcerting, but Ben looks incredibly pleased as he stands to take our trash to the receptacle and says, "My lady has spoken."

Once they leave, I turn an expectant gaze toward Cooper, since he's had plenty of extra time to come up with a creative zinger.

He doesn't disappoint, when he says, "You're the orange grease on top of my pizza."

I chuckle before answering, "You're the green scum on my pond."

With that, we dive back into our rapid-fire banter. He tells me I'm the 'ant at his picnic,' so I say he's the 'cloud in my blue sky.' He fires back that I'm the 'ding on his car door,' so I respond that he's the 'smudge on my sunglasses.' When he indicates that I'm the 'dirt under his fingernails,' I tell him that he's the 'brown spot on my banana.'

Soon, we're just yelling them back and forth, not caring that the other patrons in Wendy's are starting to stare.

"Wart on my toad!"

"Rain on my parade!"

"Dead bug in my swimming pool!"

"Chunks in my milk!"

"Weed in my flower garden!"

Leaning in close and gazing directly

into my eyes, Cooper asks, "Are you as turned on as I am right now?"

I surprise us both by answering, "More."

# 6

## COOPER

We quickly decide that I'll drive Poppy to my place, then deliver her back to her car in the morning. It's the first thing we've agreed on all evening.

I take her hand as we wait for the elevator in the parking garage. Her skin is startlingly cold, so I lift it to my mouth, engulf it with both of my palms and blow hot air on it before asking, "Do you need my jacket?"

"No, I'm fine," she assures me, before adding, "My hands and feet are always icy cold. Poor circulation, I guess. But you know what they always say… cold hands, warm heart."

"Hmm," I murmur noncommittally as we step onto the elevator and I push the button for the correct floor.

If anyone had told me when Poppy swooped in to steal my parking spot that I would end the evening by taking her to my place, I would have laughed them out of town, but something about the bristly woman is absolutely intriguing.

She further proves that after climbing into my car and saying, "There is one thing I need to know before I spend the night with you…" At my raised brows, she asks, "Do you have coffee?"

I chuckle at the absurd question, before answering, "Absolutely. What kind of barbarian do you take me for?"

As I back out of the parking spot, she deadpans, "You never know these days. There are some crazies out there. Speaking of which, it's not decaf, right?"

I give an exaggerated shiver before saying, "No, I've never understood the point of drinking decaf coffee."

"I know, right?" she quickly agrees.

It's quiet for a long moment as I drive us toward my home on Geist Reservoir. Revealing the first chink in her impressive armor, Poppy asks in a serious tone, "You don't really hate me, do you, Cooper?"

Surprised that she has shown this vulnerability, I answer, "No more than you hate me."

"Hmm." The uncertain sound emits from her closed lips as she ponders my answer. Evidently deciding that works, she says, "Okay, then."

When I pull into the driveway of my sprawling, brick home, she says, "Nice pad. What do you do for a living?"

Wishing I had a more impressive-sounding job, I answer, "I'm an investment broker, so I spend the vast majority of my time handling other people's money."

"Looks like you've managed to handle some of your own, too," she weighs in as she shifts in her seat.

It's an odd statement. An awkward tension arises in the car as I park in my garage. I try to make light of it by saying, "It seems like we're more comfortable together when we're insulting each other."

"Indeed," she agrees as she reaches for her door handle.

"I'll come around and get that for you," I offer, trying to be a gentleman.

"No need," she answers, as she opens her own door and climbs out of my car.

I mutter under my breath, "Stubborn woman."

She evidently hears me because she says, "I've been called worse."

As I turn to lead her into my home, I answer, "I'm sure you have."

After we walk into my kitchen, we stand there gaping at each other. The sexual tension that had built up while we were bickering at Wendy's seems to have completely dissipated.

In an attempt to charm her and get us back on track, I say, "I think maybe we've been destined to be together since that first moment when we locked gazes and scowled at each other over that parking space. We just didn't know it yet."

She has the audacity to scoff at me before asking, "Does that kind of cheesy line ever work for you?"

"Yes, every time," I assure her before adding, "so don't be the single mar on my perfect record."

"I hate to break it to you, but you're not nearly as charming as you obviously believe yourself to be," she says, looking like she doesn't actually hate breaking the news to me at all.

"You know, I've always heard that there is a thin line between love and hate. Do you believe that could be true?"

"Perhaps," she answers. After mulling it over for a moment, she adds, "I guess we're going to find out."

Awkwardness begins to set in again, so

I ask, "Are you thirsty? Would you like a beverage?"

"I could use some ice water," she answers, so I head over to the cabinet to retrieve a glass for her.

When she takes the glass out of my hand, I offer, "I'll get it for you."

"I think I can find where you keep the ice," she tells me as she heads to the freezer to help herself.

As she takes several large gulps of her chilled water, I wonder if she's as nervous as I am. She proves that she might be by turning to me and saying, "I can be extremely difficult to get along with because I'm always right about everything."

I grin at her before answering, "What a coincidence... because I'm never wrong about anything. I can see why Phoebe's app matched us. Sounds like we should be super compatible."

Our gazes lock together as we share a quiet moment of amusement over how wrong we obviously are for each other.

"Not everyone thinks it's worth the trouble to break through my walls, and that's okay. They're wrong, though. I am worth the work, but I tend to think there are two ways to go about everything––my way and the wrong way," she tells me.

Believing her and deciding to be vulnerable, I say, "It's clear that we both have stubborn and obnoxious streaks. We will probably bicker nonstop, but I think we owe it to ourselves to see if this can turn into something real. My guess is that we will discover a fiery passion burning between us that isn't like anything either of us have ever experienced before."

"Perhaps," she says, before adding, "But what if we end up wanting to strangle each other?"

I shrug my shoulders before asking her, "Or what if we end up falling madly in love?"

"It would be unfortunate timing because I've been intending to take a mancation to allow me to focus all of my attention on my artwork," she says as if falling in love would ruin her grand plans.

"The men of the world would appreciate that," I say, without thinking–– quickly falling back into the comfortable pattern of firing insults at her. When she angles a narrow-eyed glare in my direction, I add, "I didn't mean that. There's just something about you that brings out this unfamiliar, primal, and aggressive side of me."

She sets her glass down and steps forward into my personal space before suggesting in a husky voice, "Show me more, you sexy savage."

Happy to oblige, I lean down and crush my lips to hers.

## 7

## POPPY

My hot and cold feelings for Cooper don't make a lick of sense. One minute I want to clobber him, and the next, I'm desperate to cling to him in the throes of passion. I've never felt this burning need for anyone, and it's terrifying.

His tantalizing kiss is bold and confident. It is filled with an irresistible fervency that leaves me aching for more. He brings his warm palms to the sides of my face, cradling my cheeks like I am the most precious being he's ever encountered.

I moan into his mouth as our tongues find each other and slowly slide together, mimicking the sensuous tango our bodies long to engage in. He keeps kissing me senseless as one of his hands begins exploring the bare skin that my one-shouldered dress leaves exposed.

His finger trails a tantalizingly slow line down the side of my neck, along my collarbone, across my shoulder, and down the entire length of my arm––all the way to my fingertips. That simple touch creates a vibrating tingle in its wake that makes the tiny hairs along my arm stand up and prickle with awareness.

My free hand comes up to rub his scruffy jawline. His short beard tickles my palms in a most delightful way. I'm convinced this has to be as good as it gets when he proves me wrong by leaning down to lightly nuzzle those bristles along my neck as he presses sweet kisses to my sensitive skin.

Needing to feel more of him, my fingers begin working to unbutton his dark dress shirt. As soon as I have the tiny buttons free, I ease my palms down over his smooth chest and along the sides of his flat abdomen.

He sucks a breath in through his teeth at my touch. I immediately yank my hands back and say, "Sorry."

When he leans back to look into my eyes, I immediately miss his exquisite kisses and exploration of me. His expression is perplexed when he asks, "What are you sorry for?"

"I know my hands are freezing. I won't touch you, if you don't want me to." I stare down at the tile floor, balling my hands into fists and willing them to warm up, even though I know it's a lost cause.

He reaches out to lift my chin with his finger. Once I'm looking at him, he says, "The coldness startled me a bit at first, but it feels wonderful. Put your hands back on me. Now."

The gruff, firm order surprises me, but I like this take-charge, commanding side of him. As much as I enjoy being bossy about everything else, there's no denying how titillating it is to be ordered around by an alpha male in the bedroom.

Obeying him, I use my chilly hands to slide his open shirt over his shoulders and let it fall to the floor. He rewards me by reaching up to unbutton the three buttons on my right shoulder that are holding my dress up. Once he has them unhooked, he slowly lowers the fabric.

I hadn't been able to wear a bra with the single-shoulder dress, so the cool air teases my skin as he peels down the upper half of my dress.

He leans back to take in the sight of my bare breasts. My chest heaves as I try to keep my breathing under control. His half-lidded, desirous gaze makes heat spread out from my chest like warm liquid.

In a flash, he lunges in my direction. His hands clasp my ass and lift me onto the marble countertop of his large kitchen island. Almost immediately, one breast is engulfed by his large, rough hand and the other is in his hot, wet mouth.

My head tips back at the sudden electrifying currents pulsing through me as he worships my boobs. My hands find their way to the back of his neck, and I arch my back––silently granting him even more access.

His finger and thumb have rolled one nipple into a hard, aching nub. When his teeth lightly graze the other, I cry out–– stunned by how good this feels, yet desperate for more.

Seeming to sense my urgency, Cooper's hands find the hem of my dress. He slides his palms up my legs and over the outer edges of my thighs, taking my skirt up with them. When he reaches my hips, he hooks his fingers over the sides of my panties.

His mouth pauses from lavishing attention on my breast long enough for him to growl, "Lift that delectable ass."

I scramble to comply, and he quickly slides my panties down my legs. When he reaches my high heels, he massages each ankle before gently taking my fancy shoes off and gingerly setting them on the floor. I appreciate the care he takes with my heels, since they're the most expensive shoes I own.

Without the barrier of my pumps to stop them, my lacy panties fall further down. I point my toes to kick them off and immediately forget about them when Cooper reaches down to find me wet and ready for him.

After lifting my dress over my head and tossing it aside, he demands, "Lie back on the counter."

Although it crosses my mind that it's a bit obscene to sprawl out naked on the kitchen counter of a man I just met and bickered with all evening, I can't bring myself to truly care. I'm far too excited to see what sensual surprises he has in store for me.

I lean up on one elbow to watch him kick off his leather loafers and surprisingly gaudy dress socks. When he reaches for his belt buckle, the sound of the metal unclasping makes me swallow audibly. I'm so keyed up with nerves and anticipation, I can hardly stand the wait as he unfastens his pants and slowly lowers the zipper.

He saves time by removing his pants and underwear in one swift, smooth move. When he stands back up, my eyes are drawn to his cock. It's truly impressive, and it's probing out in my direction as if seeking my touch.

Unable to resist teasing him a bit, I say, "You saw my Mini Cooper tonight at the bar's parking lot. I'm thrilled to get to meet your--"

He interrupts me to say, "Please don't use the word 'mini' in reference to my junk."

We both chuckle because his manhood is anything but small. When I shift to reach a hand out toward him, he turns serious and says in a no-nonsense tone, "No touching me, until you're coming undone with the need for me."

It's tempting to tell him that I'm already nearly there, but I merely gaze back at him with wide eyes as I nod my head in agreement to his wonderful plan.

He spreads my legs apart and steps

forward. The heat of him radiates near my core as he lifts one of my legs, kisses along my inner thigh up toward the apex, then hooks my leg over his shoulder. After giving my other leg the same scintillating treatment, I'm left open before him.

He gazes at me as if my body is the greatest gift he's ever received. When he turns to the side to kiss and lick his way along my legs, my hips thrust up in desperation for him to put his mouth where I need it most.

My eyes glaze over when the hot air from his mouth greets me as he hovers just above where I want him. I dig my heels into his shoulders and beg him, "Please."

"Please what?" the frustrating man asks.

"Please put your mouth on me," I clarify between desperate pants.

"My mouth is on you," he murmurs between delectable kisses of my inner thigh. At my anguished cry, he instructs me, "Tell me exactly what you want."

My head thrashes back and forth as all sense of propriety and decency slip away. All that matters is that man's talented mouth and what I ache for him to do to my body. Not caring a bit that I will likely be mortified in the morning that I shouted this during the throes of passion, I yell, "I need your mouth on my pussy!"

He rewards my enthusiastic obedience by lowering his face to the place I crave him most and devouring me.

## 8

## COOPER

*P*oppy is so responsive and delectable. I could lick her sweet pussy for hours, but she's already close to coming. Her legs are quivering beside my ears and she's thrusting her body up into my mouth as she moans incoherently. My swish, flick, sucking rhythm has her teetering on the edge of oblivion.

I want to make her come undone so hard that she'll never think about another man ever again. I need to make her mine––all mine.

After my hands brush down her sides, they move around to cup her ass cheeks, lifting her higher as I feast on her. She trembles as my tongue laps greedily at her opening.

Her fingernails claw into the skin at

the back of my neck as she gasps and pulses up into me. She screams my name as I love the core of her sex with increased vigor.

She's panting when she finally lifts her head up to look at me. I stand and her gaze travels down to my hard cock. She licks her lips before whispering in a husky voice, "I need you inside me."

Fully on board with that plan, I help her sit up as I say, "That's the best idea you've had all night."

She wraps her legs tightly around me as I lift her. Reaching down, she lines my tip up with her slick opening. We gaze into each other's eyes as she slowly slides down the length of me, taking me in all the way to the hilt.

Her hot, wet pussy surrounds me, and I'm lost in the ecstasy of being buried inside her. My knees want to buckle with pleasure, but I force them not to give out on us. Instead, I turn to carry her to my bedroom.

My walking creates hip thrusts that spurn Poppy on. She tips her head back and begins riding my cock as I try to take steps. Soon, the bedroom is no longer a viable option. I focus on getting to the hall carpeting, since it will make a better cushion for us than the kitchen tile.

I make it to the hall's threshold, but just barely. As I gently lower Poppy to the floor, I grunt in explanation, "I need you now."

Proving that she's completely on board with banging on the floor in my hallway, Poppy breathes out the word, "Yes."

As soon as she is safely settled onto the plush carpet I rear back and drive all the way inside her. A deep, primal groan emerges from my throat as the warm satisfaction of being engulfed by her washes through me.

I straighten my arms and gaze down at her as I rotate my hips to find the right stroke to maximize her pleasure. When her eyes roll back in her head, I continue with that rhythm as she meets me thrust for thrust. The delectable friction as we move together creates a coiling pressure inside me that demands release.

Her head thrashes from side to side as her slick pussy begins tightening around me. I reach down between us to give her clit a few quick flicks. That light touch is enough to send her crashing over the edge of the cliff.

She moans and clenches around my cock, grinding her body up into me. The squeezing sensation makes my body go rigid. My teeth graze her collarbone as the pleasure becomes too much for me to contain.

The uncontrollable spiral of release begins as my pumping hips pick up speed. Poppy reaches back to grab my ass cheeks--enthusiastically pulling me into her. Our heated bodies slap together as I let go. A guttural moan escapes my open mouth as the orgasm zings through my body, electrifying my limbs and leaving me spent.

When I flop my weight on top of her, she lightly trails her fingernails down my back before saying, "That line between love and hate might be even thinner than we thought."

I chuckle at the delightful woman before agreeing, "Indeed."

## 9

## POPPY

*A*fter rocking my world with some of the best sex I've had in… well, forever, Cooper tenderly picks me up and carries me to his bed. He curls protectively around me and almost immediately begins lightly snoring. I've never felt so cherished or adored. It's both wonderful and a bit frightening.

My eyelids drift closed for a moment and when they flutter open, it's a new day. Streaks of sunshine are just starting to slash across the plush carpet in his bedroom, and my stupid insecurities begin to flare. Insults and arguments can't possibly be the foundation for a long-term, healthy relationship. *Can they?*

We would both likely be better off with someone we actually get along with. The thought makes my head pound. Or perhaps, it's my lack of caffeine. Either way, it's time to get moving.

There isn't a viable way for me to get out of Cooper's strong embrace without waking him, so I bend my knees and place the bottoms of my icy feet on his legs.

He stiffens immediately. His voice sounds sleepy and endearing when he says, "That's one way to wake me up."

Deciding that I may as well be my true self right from the start, I grumble, "Need coffee."

His eyes are barely open, but he snorts out a chuckle and moves to get up. "As you wish, my lady."

I make a quick pit stop in the bathroom. He delivers last night's dress to the door for me to put on. When I head out to the kitchen, the scent of freshly brewed coffee greets me, so I pause to breathe it in as he pours me the first cup.

He has pulled on some loose gray sweatpants that showcase the tiny, delectable indentations at his hips. As he hands me the steaming mug, he asks, "Did you sleep okay?"

I blow on the tasty brew before saying, "Let the magic beans do their work before you speak to me."

He smiles and nods before pouring himself a cup. I take my first sip of the delicious black coffee and let the heat spread through my veins before admitting, "Some days I'm tempted to skip the cup and drink directly from the pot."

After he runs a hand through his adorably sleep-rumpled hair, he says, "You're even more addicted to this stuff than I am. I didn't think that was possible."

"It's what keeps me going all day in the studio," I tell him.

He swallows the first drink from his mug. In a curious tone, he asks me, "What kind of art do you do?"

"Stained glass," I answer quickly. Deciding that response is a bit abrupt, I add, "That medium allows me to release my anger by breaking things, then I get to force the shards to morph together into something beautiful."

"Sounds perfect for you," he weighs in using a thoughtful tone. Quickly changing gears and pushing off the counter to walk away, he says, "Make yourself at home. I need to go shower for work. I'll drop you off at your car on my way to the office. I should still be able to make it on time."

He glances down at his phone to confirm before hurrying down the hallway. Unwilling to admit how miffed I am that he didn't invite me into his shower, I mutter quietly to myself, "Great, I'll just sit here and wait, then."

When he returns to the kitchen, a delectable, masculine scent wafts into the room in his wake. He is wearing a dark gray suit, his hair is damp, and his face is clean-shaven. I'd like to see how smooth it would feel against my skin, but he ruins that idea by asking, "Ready to go?"

I'd been half-expecting him to offer to make me a hot breakfast––or at least toast––so his urgency to get rid of me is a bit jarring. Trying not to show my hurt feelings, I grab my purse and say, "Oh, okay. Sure."

Seeming to sense that he's been too abrupt, he says, "Sorry, but I don't want to be late for work. I can't stand running behind."

"Yet another thing we don't have in common. I don't really pay much attention to time." I give him a sad smile as I realize that we truly are opposites in every way.

Once we're settled in his car, I glance down and do a double-take before saying, "Nice socks."

Last night, I'd thought perhaps his colorful socks were a fluke or something special for his Man of the Month Club debut, but the smiling bright yellow bananas peeking out between the hem of his gray slacks and dress shoes this morning make it obvious that this is a deliberate style choice.

He turns to grin at me as he starts the car, seeming pleased that I have noticed. "My investment firm job is so boring, I needed to find some small way to bring some levity into it. I have three drawers full of outlandish and fun statement socks."

"Living on the edge," I quip. Despite my sarcastic comment, I grin down at my lap as I think how charming it is that he's obviously so proud of his 'wild' streak.

Once he backs out of his driveway and wheels the car onto his street, he points out the beautiful home next door and says, "Beau Wallace, the Indy race car driver lives there."

"Really?" I ask with more enthusiasm in my tone than I intend. Impressed despite myself, I try not to gush as I add, "He seems like such a great guy whenever he does television interviews. I was devastated when I saw he had that bad accident at last year's Indy 500."

"Yeah, that was really scary watching him hit the wall. He had gotten me tickets for the race, so I was at the track." His voice has taken on a somber tone, but it brightens when he adds, "It's been almost a year, though, and he's doing surprisingly well––considering the circumstances. He got really lucky."

I shake my head as I say, "I can't believe your next-door neighbor is *the* Beau Wallace."

He nods and angles a quick smile in my direction before saying, "He's a great neighbor, except he has a tendency to speed on our little side streets."

I chuckle as I picture the racer trying to abide by the luxurious neighborhood's ironic 14 ½ mile per hour speed limit signs.

Silence settles over the car as we drive toward the bar's parking lot, until Cooper asks me, "What is your family like?"

I'd been hoping to avoid this topic, but since he asked, I'm blatantly honest with my answer. "It's really just me and my mom. She had me at a very young age, so she thinks I ruined her life. We don't have much of a relationship."

I leave out the fact that her hatred of me is the main reason I'm so wildly insecure about personal relationships. It's been ingrained into my personality from an early age not to believe that anyone can truly love me, so I end up pushing people away before they try to get close.

The one exception to that is my best friend, Daphne. Somehow, she has been able to break down my walls, and I let her in. It's probably because she is so pure and loving that my heart knows there is no way she could ever hurt me. But she's the only person I trust like that.

Part of me wonders if I might someday be able to trust Cooper enough to let him inside, but the mere idea of it makes my heart hammer in my chest. It would be easier to keep him at a safe distance until we see if we both want to pursue a relationship with each other.

All too soon, we pull into the nearly empty parking lot.

"Primo parking spot," Cooper grumbles as he pulls in beside my car.

Deciding to take the high road, I opt not to point out that I won it fair and square. Instead, I say sincerely, "I had a great time last night."

"Me, too." His voice is husky, but he doesn't ask to see me again.

Trying to hide my crushed feelings from my facial expression, I give him a brittle smile and say, "Okay, then. Goodbye."

"That's it?" he asks, sounding hurt.

When I turn to see what he means, he takes the opportunity to crush his lips to mine. I respond immediately to his possessive kiss--moaning into his mouth and threading my fingers through the hair at the nape of his neck.

After we finally pull apart, I reach for my door handle and say, "I'm not sure how steady on my feet I'll be after that."

"Good," he responds, sounding proud. "That will give you something to think about until I can get my hands on you again."

Beaming and not bothering to cover my significant delight, I say, "Can't wait."

# COOPER

*T*he text from Phoebe to both Poppy and me sounds urgent. *"Can we meet tonight for dinner? I have something important to tell you both."*

Poppy and I both respond that we are available, so Phoebe sends us the address of one of my favorite local pizzerias and asks us to meet her there at 6:00 p.m.

I arrive a few minutes early, of course, and am surprised to see Poppy already seated at a table for four. After sliding in beside her on the red leather booth, I lean in to kiss her cheek before saying, "You're early."

"It happens once in a great while," she says. Her tone turns more serious when she adds, "Especially when I'm nervous. Do you have any idea what Phoebe wants?"

"Nope," I answer nonchalantly. When I see the tiny worry-line emerge between Poppy's eyebrows as she stares down at the red and white checkered tablecloth, I try to distract her by asking, "What do you like on your pizza?"

"Sausage and pepperoni," she answers immediately.

"No way! That's exactly what I always get. We actually have something in common. I guess we truly are made for each other," I say.

I'd been teasing, but the furrow grows deeper between her brows when she says, "Liking the same toppings on our pizza doesn't mean anything."

"It's a start," I assure her as I take her hand within mine. I'd been expecting hers to be chilly, but it's clammy and damp, too––making me wonder why she's so nervous.

Before I can ask her about it, Phoebe arrives at the booth with a pretty blonde woman by her side. The two of them sit down across from us as Phoebe says, "Oh, good. You're both already here."

With impeccable timing, our waitress shows up to take our drink order. After we make our requests, I ask for an order of garlic knots for the table, and the harried woman rushes off.

ANN OMASTA & CALLIE LOVE

Wanting to make sure our order is set for when the waitress returns with our drinks, I ask the other two women, "Do you like sausage and pepperoni pizza, or would you like to get something else?"

Phoebe nods her agreement and the blonde says, "That's my favorite!"

Poppy angles a look at me, and I can practically hear her saying, "I told you it wasn't a sign," even though she remains quiet. Not wanting her to focus on that, I turn my attention to Phoebe and ask, "So, what's up?"

The tall woman leans in to say, "Well, we all saw last night what a mismatch the two of you are. So, I stayed up all night trying to figure out how the app could have gotten things so wrong, and I found a bug in the algorithm!"

She says this as if it is great news, even though it's not at all what I want to hear. Poppy stiffens at my side, and I can tell this is going to hit her hard.

"I'm so sorry I didn't catch it sooner," Phoebe rushes on, not seeming to sense how upsetting her news is. "I could have saved the two of you from having a terrible date. It's too late for that, but I wanted to make things right as soon as possible."

I'm shaking my head, willing her to

stop talking, but she continues on—obviously oblivious to the dagger she is jabbing into my heart. "Coop, you shouldn't have been matched with Poppy at all. Your best match is Summer."

She indicates the blonde by her side, before beaming at me with a wide smile as if this is great news.

Poppy deflates beside me before plastering on a fake smile and saying, "That's great! You two will be terrific together."

Before I can object, she begins pushing on my shoulder to try to make her way out of the booth. I don't budge.

"I'm going to head out. My belly isn't feeling quite right, so I don't want any pizza," she says, even though she hadn't mentioned anything about an upset stomach earlier.

When I see the tears welling in her eyes, I'm torn about what to do. I don't want to let her leave like this, but I know she'll be mortified if she cries in front of us.

"Let me out!" she demands with vigor in her voice, despite its shakiness.

I startle us all by saying just as firmly, "No."

11

## POPPY

*I* don't see what this annoying, stubborn man isn't understanding. Speaking as if he's a five-year-old, I say, "I'm not a match with you. Summer is your match. The two of you need to go on a date to see if you're as compatible as the app says you will be."

When I try again to move him aside, so I can escape to my car and cry, he remains planted in his seat. At my angry huff, he says firmly, "You're not going anywhere, until you hear what I have to say."

The waitress arrives with our red plastic drink cups and a basket filled with piping hot garlic knots. They would probably smell delectable, if I wasn't so upset. Cooper places our pizza order and the woman hurries away as Phoebe and Summer both reach for rolls.

Both women lean in and munch on the knots as if they are as anxious to see what Cooper has to say as I am. He turns his attention to them to say in a no-nonsense tone, "Phoebe, your app is wrong."

When she starts to agree, he holds his palm up to add, "It's wrong now. Summer, no offense, but I don't want to go out with you. You are beautiful, and I'm sure you'll make someone very happy, but it won't be me. I've already found my love match, and she's sitting right beside me."

He turns to look deeply into my eyes and steals my breath away. My eyelashes flutter rapidly as I struggle to take in this wonderful, surprising turn of events.

Taking my chilly hands within his warm ones, he says, "Poppy, you are the one for me. Perhaps it was destiny for us to be mismatched. I don't know the reason, and I don't care. All that matters is I choose you, and I hope you'll choose me."

He seems to be expecting an answer, but I don't trust my voice, so I merely nod.

"I don't want to date anyone else because you're not just a woman. You're *the* woman for me." After that wonderful proclamation, Cooper leans in to press his lips to mine.

Some portion of my brain registers that our pizza is being delivered, but I can't bring myself to care. All that matters is Cooper's captivating kiss.

When we finally, reluctantly break apart, Summer claps her hands and squeals, "Oh, this is so romantic! I knew from your auras that the two of you were a wondrous match."

I grin at the excited woman in the gauzy, flower-patterned dress. She truly seems happy for us. I can't even imagine because if I had been Cooper's true match, and he chose someone else, I'd be seething with jealousy.

Just as I'm deciding I might actually like this hippy-dippy person, she turns wide eyes to Phoebe to ask, "What should we make their ship name––Coppy or Pooper?"

Leaning across the table, I say in a firm tone, "How about no?"

All three of the others chuckle at my bristly reaction.

Since my stomach issue has completely dissipated, I grab a slice of pizza and take a huge bite.

Phoebe seizes the opportunity to say sheepishly, "Our Man of the Month Club group is really starting to take off, so perhaps we could all keep quiet about this slight mishap––err, happy mistake––with the application?"

Summer and I nod our agreement as Cooper stares directly at me to answer Phoebe's question. "As long as I get to live happily ever after with the woman of my dreams, your secret is safe with me."

## EPILOGUE: POPPY

*A*s we climb into Cooper's car, I say, "I know running late stresses you out. I'm sorry I couldn't keep my hands off you this morning."

He angles a knowing look at me before saying, "It wasn't like I was fighting you off."

It's tempting to point out that it's his own fault for being so damn irresistible, but I opt to take the high road instead. "You told me we had a couple of stops to make before our appointment, but I joined you in the shower anyway."

"Don't ever blame yourself for that. I could have hurried things along, but I chose to take my time and love you properly. If anyone's to blame, it's my fault we're running a bit late."

Tipping up one side of my mouth to

angle an ornery grin at him, I say, "You're right. I'll let you win this one... It's your fault."

His guffaw of laughter echoes inside the car as he reverses out of the driveway.

"Are you going to tell me where we're going?" I ask.

"First, we're stopping to pick up another woman," he hints.

I don't particularly like the sound of that, but I know I can trust him. We turn out of his neighborhood adjacent to the water, and he makes an immediate left into the driveway of a small, rundown home that doesn't match the sprawling estates that surround it.

A tiny, hunch-backed woman clutching a leather handbag with both hands bustles quickly outside as if she has been standing at the door waiting for us.

Cooper gets out and hurries around to the passenger's side of the vehicle. Not wanting the older woman to have to climb into the backseat of the car, I open my door to move back there. Once he sees what I'm up to, Cooper holds out a hand to help me out of his vehicle.

The shriveled woman stops and squints up at me before turning to Cooper and saying, "Oh, you have a lady friend with you. No wonder you're late."

Scrunching up her wrinkled face, she adds, "And here I thought I was the only one for you."

Cooper gallantly brings the back of her liver spot covered hand up to his lips before saying, "You'll always be my first love, Mrs. Richards, but today is my lucky day because I get to drive two beauties around town."

The woman cackles happily before waggling a crooked finger at me to say, "You're a pretty one. Pretty girls usually cause trouble. My sweet Cooper has the biggest heart of any young man I've ever known. If you hurt him, you'll have to deal with me."

"Understood," I say, nodding my head solemnly, before adding, "I won't hurt him."

Mrs. Richards must sense my sincerity because she nods her head before moving around me to get to the car's back door. I quickly offer, "You can ride in the front. I'll sit in the back."

She glares up at me before saying, "We both know he would rather sit beside you."

Cooper helps get her settled in the backseat and closes her door before whispering to me, "She's right, you know. I want you by my side—always."

A delightful tingle shivers down my spine at his wonderful words as I slide into the front seat of his car, before he closes the door for me.

As he walks around to the driver's side, the woman in the backseat says, "He's a true gentleman, and that's a rarity these days. If you're as smart as you look, you'll hold onto him."

"I intend to," I assure her just before he rejoins us in the car.

Cooper puts on the oldies radio station as we drive. Soon, all three of us are bopping our heads, humming, and singing to the classic, upbeat tunes.

After Cooper pulls into a parking space at the ladies' beauty shop, he turns to me to say loud enough for the other woman to hear, "You think Georgia is pretty now, but wait until you see how beautiful she looks when we pick her up."

The woman actually titters at his compliment, before leaning forward to hand him a neatly folded dollar bill. "You'll be back here to pick me up in two hours?"

"You can count on me," he assures her as he accepts the money and tucks it into his pocket as if it is a great prize.

I watch from the car as he escorts her inside the salon. Through the picture window, I see him bend down to kiss the older woman on the cheek before turning to leave.

Once he's back in the car, I say, "That is easily the sweetest thing I've ever witnessed, but she's probably on a very limited budget. Why do you let her pay you?"

"I used to argue with her about taking the money, but she's a proud woman, and she likes to feel like she is paying her own way," he answers as he backs out of our parking spot.

Understanding that urge, I say, "That makes sense."

Once he wheels us out on the road, he reaches over to hold my hand as he drives. I savor the connection with him as I ask, "How often do you bring her to get her hair done?"

"Every Saturday morning," he answers.

I stare at his gorgeous profile, unable to believe how impossibly sweet and caring he is. Choosing to be vulnerable, I say, "You're making it damn hard not to fall madly in love with you, Cooper Bridgerton."

He pulls his gaze from the road for a second to give me an ornery grin as he says, "That's the plan."

When he pulls into a parking lot next to a line of renovated brick buildings downtown, I ask, "What are we doing here?"

"You'll see," he answers mysteriously as he practically lunges from the car.

He takes my hand and hurries me toward one of the storefronts. The elegant real estate broker already has the door open, so she ushers us inside with a swoosh of her hand.

Confused, I turn to ask Cooper, "What am I looking at?"

"I've never felt fulfilled by my boring financial job. It's lucrative, but it isn't my passion," he starts.

I remain quiet, beyond curious to hear what he *is* passionate about.

"The only tiny bit of fun I've managed to insert into my workdays is my stupid statement socks. But it's those colorful additions to my otherwise gray world at work, along with your beautiful cut glass pieces, that have inspired me to follow my heart."

The real estate broker pretends to focus on her phone as she steps outside to give us some privacy.

I'm staring at him with wide eyes as he says, "I've leased this space, and I'm going to open an affordable art studio where the average Joe can purchase a beautiful piece of artwork to display and brighten up his home. I'd like to commission some of your artwork, if you're willing, and I'll get Ben on board to show a few of his drawings. With consignments from fantastic artists like the two of you, I'm sure it won't take long for the gallery to take off."

I turn in a full circle, picturing the place filled with beautiful, vivid artwork that is reasonably priced for the non-millionaires of the world.

Showing the first hint of insecurity, Cooper sounds apprehensive when he asks, "What do you think? Is this crazy? Have I lost my mind?"

Wanting to reassure him, I rush into his arms before answering, "I think it's wonderful, and it's going to be a smashing success. I love you, Coop."

He gazes down at me with a look that makes me melt before saying, "I love you, too, Pop."

"Nope," I tell him firmly.

"Come on, I think it's an adorable nickname," he tries.

"It's a hard pass," I say.

"Then it will never cross my lips again, my lady," he assures me, before pressing his mouth down to mine in a toe-curling kiss that holds the precious promise of forever.

~

PEACEFUL, free-spirited Summer Flynn is the last person anyone expected to be paired with angry, tough-guy Killian Jenkins, but the Man of the Month Club matchmaking application is full of surprises. Read on for a sneak peek of their story, *Man of the Month Club: JUNE*.

~

CURIOUS ABOUT COOPER'S fast-driving neighbor, Beau? Read his second-chance, amnesia romance in *His First Time: Beau*.

# SNEAK PEEK MAN OF
# THE MONTH CLUB: JUNE
# (SUMMER)

---

*P*hoebe's nervous energy tonight is practically vibrating off her in visible waves. My bracelets jangle as I reach out to clasp her clammy hand within my warm one. I focus on channeling my calming energy to her as I practice the Reiki healing touch technique that I've been learning during my classes at the recreation center.

Proving that I still have more work to do in that particular class, Phoebe snatches her hand back and says, "I'm really worried about tonight's match, Summer."

"I can see that." I say the words quietly before asking her, "Would you like to talk about it?"

We're the only two people at the table so far. I rode to the bar for this month's meeting with her, since my old, beater car is at the repair shop––again. It almost seems like Rusty from Rusty's Garage sees my aging, silver Volkswagen Beetle more than I do, but I love that car so much, I can't imagine selling. It's been too vital a part of my life to get rid of it.

Phoebe studies me for a long moment before saying, "I've been really worried about this month's bachelor. He's not our typical successful businessman-type."

"That might be a good thing. Not everyone is looking for a working-stiff drone," I assure her.

"Right, but this guy is…" She pauses for a long moment and bites her lip as she searches for the right description. She finally lands on, "Rough around the edges."

"I'm sure he'll be fine. After all, he was a high-compatibility match with someone, right?"

"Yes, but…" Phoebe pauses again as if she is afraid of saying too much.

I keep my gaze steady on her, even when she averts her eyes and begins staring down at the table before trying again to explain, "He's a great guy, but…"

"What is it?" I ask her, gently urging her to confide in me before the other ladies begin arriving.

Finally, the words rush from Phoebe's

mouth in a flourish. "I'm afraid this month's match is all wrong. These two people couldn't be more opposite, and I know that sometimes opposites attract, but these are *extreme* opposites. Their approaches to life couldn't be more different."

She pauses to glance around and make sure we're still alone before whispering, "And after last month's fiasco, I'm really worried that the app has somehow gone off the rails. Our reputation is really starting to build, but one horrid match could ruin all of that fantastic momentum we've been amassing for the official launch."

"One bad match doesn't prove anything," I assure her, trying my best to calm her jitters.

I am one of only a handful of people who know about the glitch that kept me from being paired with Cooper Bridgerton last month. Phoebe had been mortified by the mistake, but I am convinced the Universe stepped in to make things work out as they were meant to with May's match.

Besides, even though Cooper is handsome and charming, I know he isn't the right man for me. Something about our vibe together felt off, but I can't explain that to Phoebe. She already thinks I'm a flower child hippy. Telling her about wonky vibes would only confirm that impression. Even though it might be somewhat accurate, there's more to me than flowing dresses and meditation, and I'd like for people to start recognizing that.

"Everything will work out for the best... I promise," I tell her, fully believing that the Universe has a plan for all of us.

Suddenly, the feeling of calm that normally pervades my senses dissipates as my attention is drawn by the hulking man that is standing at our table. My hand flutters to my throat as his commanding presence seems to suck all of the fresh air out of the room.

I gawk up at the huge, tattoo-covered biceps that are peeking out of his tight, black T-shirt. His waist tapers to a tantalizing vee that leads down to perfectly fitting black jeans, which conceal a hefty-looking bulge at his crotch. Forcing my gaze back up, my throat goes dry as I'm overwhelmed by his intense, dark stare.

Breaking her own rule of secrecy until the official reveal to the group, Phoebe leans over and whispers to me, "This is June's bachelor, Killian, and you've been matched with him."

I swallow audibly as I drink in the

sight of the sexiest, scariest man I've ever encountered.

~

PEACEFUL, free-spirited Summer Flynn is the last person anyone expected to be paired with angry, tough-guy Killian Jenkins, but the Man of the Month Club matchmaking application is full of surprises. Will these two extreme opposites be able to meet in the middle? Or did the app make a terrible mismatch this month? Find out when you read *Man of the Month Club: JUNE*.

# LET'S STAY IN TOUCH...

*I won't let Charlotte die. I can't. She means everything to me. She needs me to stay calm and talk her through landing the plane. We can't let her find out this is my first time doing this, too.*

Ranger and Charlotte's sizzling story is FREE when you join Callie Love's VIP reader group. It's a reader group EXCLUSIVE and isn't available anywhere else. We value your privacy and never send spam. Just visit callielove.com and tell us where to send your Hot Shot of Romance Quickie.

# ACKNOWLEDGMENTS

A HUGE thank you to:

- Megan Parker, EmCat Designs (Cover artist)

- Dana Lee, Lee Clarity Consulting (Editing/Proofreading)

- The wonderful members of Ann's Clan, Ann's Amazing Aces, Ann Omasta's Reader Group, and Callie Love's Reader Group. We wouldn't be able to do what we love without you!

*Man of the Month Club: May* © copyright May 2021 by
Ann Omasta and Callie Love

Copyright notice: All rights reserved under the
International and Pan-American Copyright
Conventions. No part of this book may be
reproduced or transmitted in any form or by any
means, electronic or mechanical, including
photocopying, recording, or by any information
storage and retrieval system, without permission in
writing from the publisher.

This is a work of fiction. Names, places, characters
and incidents are either the product of the author's
imagination or are used fictitiously, and any
resemblance to any actual persons, living or dead,
organizations, events or locales is entirely
coincidental.

Warning: the unauthorized reproduction or
distribution of this copyrighted work is illegal.
Criminal copyright infringement, including
infringement without monetary gain, is investigated
by the FBI and is punishable by up to 5 years in
prison and a fine of $250,000.

❊ Created with Vellum

Printed in Dunstable, United Kingdom

69130528R10050